For Team Claude
Alison E, Alison S, Emma, and Anne

PEACHTREE PUBLISHERS
1700 Chattahoochee Avenue
Atlanta, Georgia 30318-2112
www.peachtree-online.com

Text and illustrations © 2013 by Alex T. Smith

First published in the United Kingdom in 2013 by Hodder Children's Books
First United States version published in 2014 by Peachtree Publishers
First United States trade paperback edition published in 2016

Artwork created digitally. Title is hand lettered; text is typeset in Italian Garamond BT.

Printed and bound in April 2016 in China by RR Donnelley & Sons

10 9 8 7 6 5 4 3 2 1 (hardcover)
10 9 8 7 6 5 4 3 2 1 (trade paperback)

Library of Congress Cataloging-in-Publication Data

Smith, Alex T.
  Claude on the slopes / by Alex T. Smith.
     pages cm
  Summary: Claude and his best friend, Sir Bobblysock, go to the Snowy Mountains
where they throw snowballs, learn to ski, and more until Claude's loud voice starts an
avalanche, trapping Sir Bobblysock and the only Mountain Rescue person under a huge
pile of snow.
  ISBN 978-1-56145-805-9 (hardcover) / 978-1-56145-923-0 (trade paperback)
  [1. Dogs—Fiction. 2. Socks—Fiction. 3. Snow—Fiction. 4. Avalanches—Fiction. 5.
Humorous stories.] I. Title.
  PZ7.S6422Cms 2014
  [E]—dc23
                          2014010990

CLAUDE

on the Slopes

ALEX T. SMITH

PEACHTREE
ATLANTA

Chapter 1

At 112 Waggy Avenue,
there lives a dog.

A small dog.
A small, plump dog.
A small, plump dog who
wears shoes and a sweater
and a rather nifty beret.

Rather nifty beret

Sweater

Shoes

This dog is called Claude.
Hello, Claude!

He lives with Mr. and Mrs. Shinyshoes...

...and his best pal in the whole world, Sir Bobblysock, who is both a sock and quite bobbly.

Every day, after Mr. and Mrs.
Shinyshoes have hotfooted it
out the door to work, Claude
pops on his beret and goes on
an adventure with Sir Bobblysock.

8

But where will they go next?

Chapter 2

One morning (it was a Tuesday), Claude woke up in a loud sort of a mood. He had been feeling boisterous all week.

He whistled loudly as he tied up his shoelaces. He hummed loudly as he smoothed his sweater down over his tummy.

And he said,

"Oooh! Aren't you handsome?"

loudly to himself
while looking in
a mirror.

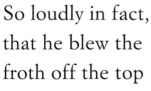

So loudly in fact,
that he blew the
froth off the top
of Sir Bobblysock's frothy coffee
from the other side of the kitchen.

Claude and Sir Bobblysock had spent the day before (which had been a Monday) at the library.

Miss Hush, the librarian, had explained that although it was okay to make a bit of noise in the library—especially when you've found a very exciting book—turning up in your one-man-band outfit was a bit much.

Jane's Hair

15 shades of beige
Your guide to paint

Peter Pan's People

·LIBRARY·

Then she had lost count of the number of times she'd had to remind Claude to use his nice Indoor Voice.

By the end of the day, Sir
Bobblysock had needed a long nap
with a damp cloth over his eyes.

But that was yesterday, and now
Claude needed a jolly new
adventure to go on.

"I think I'll go and get some
fresh air!" shouted Claude.

And he did.

15

Sir Bobblysock was hardly out of
his pajamas when Claude flung
open the front door.

"Brrr!" Claude said, shivering.
"It's ever so chill—"

But he didn't have a chance to
finish his sentence because—

Claude slipped on a patch of ice
and flew right across the street,
landing with a bump on his bottom.

Sir Bobblysock gingerly picked
his way over to see if Claude
was all right.

He was.

"What *is* all this slippery, wet, chilly stuff?" asked Claude, looking at the blanket of white that covered the street.

Then he realized—it was snow.

Claude had never seen snow for himself before, but he'd seen pictures in books. He was just wondering what to do with it all when suddenly someone *whoooooooshed* past him at a terrific speed. Then another person did. Then another.

Claude didn't know what they were doing, but he knew it was something exciting because his bottom had started to wag his tail like crazy and his eyebrows were jiggling uncontrollably.

So he ran after them
as fast as he could.

23

Claude and Sir Bobblysock followed
the whooshing people all the way to the
Snowy Mountains Winter Sports Center.

When they arrived, Claude and Sir
Bobblysock looked around with wonder.

There was so much to see!

A cozy log cabin café,

snowy mountains,

people whizzing through the air,

and people falling over.

Chapter 3

Claude had never played in the snow before, so he wasn't sure what to do. He decided just to try and join in with what other people were doing. But before he and Sir Bobblysock could do that, they needed to look the part.

Claude rummaged around in his beret. At last, Claude found just the thing tucked away behind the glitzy leotard Sir Bobblysock liked to wear to his aerobics class.

At first, Sir Bobblysock wasn't quite sure about the earmuffs, but once he'd looked at himself from every angle in Claude's mirror, he realized that they brought out the color of his eyes beautifully.

Claude and Sir Bobblysock were ready to have some fun.

The first thing they did was join in with some children who were having a snowball fight.

Claude discovered that in a snowball fight what you do is roll up some snow into a ball and throw it at other people. What you don't do is get overexcited and throw anything you find...

That goes against the spirit of
things, especially since some people
don't really enjoy getting bopped
on the head with a flying boot...

Claude said, "Sorry," and gave the boy a lollipop he found in his beret. Claude thought it would be best if he found something else to do, and besides, Sir Bobblysock wasn't very keen on all those snowballs flying around.

33

Next, the two friends discovered another group of people who were doing something unusual with what looked like a tea tray. Claude and Sir Bobblysock watched in amazement as the people zipped down the hillside. Claude thought it looked like terrific fun.

Sir Bobblysock thought
it looked very dangerous and
was sure it would make him feel
sick, so he found a place to sit
and watch, and helped himself
to a cookie.

Claude climbed to the top of the hill and asked the people what they were doing.

"We are sledding!" explained a little girl. "Do you have a tea tray you could use?"

Well, of course Claude had a tea tray he could use. He always kept one in his beret—with a full tea set just in case there was a tea-based emergency. So he whipped it out and was ready to go!

Sledding, Claude found, was
wonderful! He liked zipping down
the hill and feeling the wind in his
ears. Sir Bobblysock told him that
his ears looked lovely when they
billowed out behind him.

Soon Claude got good at
sledding and everyone said
he was a natural.

Chapter 4

But it was rather exhausting and Claude was beginning to feel a bit midmorning-ish and belly-rumbly, so he waved goodbye to his new friends and went to find Sir Bobblysock. But Sir Bobblysock was nowhere to be found.

Claude looked around and scratched his head. Then he noticed an excited-looking crowd in the distance.

"I bet Sir Bobblysock is over there!"
Claude said to himself. He knew
that his best friend was a bit of a
busybody.

Claude jogged over and, sure enough, there was Sir Bobblysock in the thick of it. He'd entered himself into the Great Snowman Competition.

THE **GREAT SNOWMAN**
COMPETITION
FABULOUS PRIZES TO BE WON!

Once, when Claude and Sir Bobblysock had been at the beach, Sir Bobblysock had discovered that he was a talented sand castle builder. And snow wasn't *that* much different from sand—that's what Sir Bobblysock thought, anyway.

44

Claude watched, hardly daring to
breathe, as Sir Bobblysock and all
the other competitors started
digging and rolling and sculpting
the snow. But Claude didn't need
to worry...

ONE SOCK
AND HIS DOG

Sir Bobblysock was a crackerjack
snow sculptor and his snowman
was definitely the best.

"Congratulations!" cried
a glamorous woman in a furry
outfit. "You are the winner!"
And she handed Sir Bobblysock
his prizes—a silver shovel and
a heated foot spa.

Claude went wild!

He whooped
and hollered in his
Outdoor Voice and
jumped up and down.

Suddenly, out of nowhere, came a swoosh of snow. Standing behind Claude and Sir Bobblysock in a brightly colored jacket and some snazzy goggles was a man on skis. He also had quite an extravagant mustache that Claude would have liked to have looked at more closely, but the man didn't look very happy, so Claude thought better of it.

Instead, he quickly put away Sir Bobblysock's prizes under his beret.

49

"My name is Sidney Snood," said the man, "and I am in charge of Mountain Rescue. You were making quite a noise then, which you really shouldn't do here."

Sidney then went on to explain that while snow was a lot of fun, it could also be very dangerous. If you made too much noise, all the snow at the top of the mountain could slip down and cover absolutely everything with more snow than was sensible.

"And that is called
an avalanche,"
said Sidney
Snood.

Claude dragged his foot around
in circles and said, "Sorry."

Then Claude told Sidney Snood how
nice he thought his mustache was.

This seemed to stop Sidney Snood
from being angry, and he smiled
a big smile.

"Would you and your friend like
to come and learn more about
Mountain Rescue?" he asked.
"Today I am doing a demonstration."

Claude nodded his head and wagged
his tail, but Sir Bobblysock wasn't
so sure. He had been hoping for a
nice sit-down and a cup of something
warm, but he hopped along behind
Claude because he always liked to
go along with his very best friend.

Chapter 5

We are going to pretend that this man has had an accident," said Sidney Snood, pointing at two legs sticking out of the snow. "I'll show you what to do."

Claude and Sir Bobblysock watched
as Sidney Snood calmly took a shovel
out from his bag and dug and dug
and dug until out came a rather
chilly looking man.

Then Sidney Snood wrapped the
man up in a special silver wrinkly
blanket and poured him a hot drink
from a thermos.

Claude had a cup of tea, too,
since it had been very hard work
supervising the rescue.

Sidney turned to Claude and Sir
Bobblysock. "So you see," he said,
"you must be careful, because this
is the kind of accident you can
cause if you use your Outdoor Voice
near snowy mountains."

"Now," continued Sidney Snood,
"would you like me to teach you
both how to ski?"

Claude was very excited and said,
"Yes, please!" But Sir Bobblysock was
worried about his bunion, so he said
he would go and find a nice cup of
tea and watch Claude from the log
cabin at the bottom of the mountains.

61

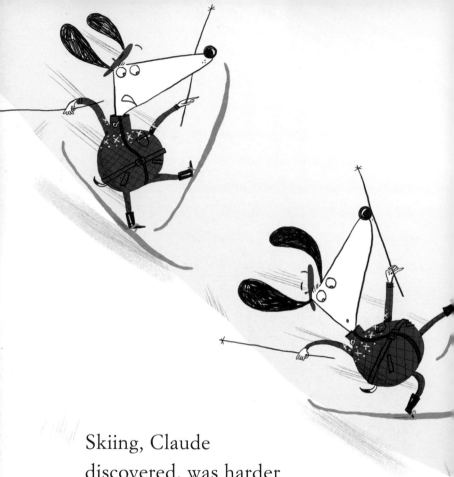

Skiing, Claude
discovered, was harder
than riding around
on a tea tray.

It was rather tricky indeed.

Sidney showed Claude how to push himself off using two sticks and how to bring his arms in close to his body so that he would move quicker.

He also showed him how to skid to a nice, calm stop. Claude found that in emergencies, using the nearest tree worked just as well.

Chapter 6

After a few fall-y down sort of tries, Claude eventually got the hang of it. He skied down a small mountain and then he skied down a medium-sized mountain.

Claude found that everyone
liked to stop and watch him.

68

"As a special treat for you being so quiet all afternoon, shall we try skiing from the top of the tallest mountain?" asked Sidney Snood.

Claude felt a bit giddy at the thought but said, "Okay," and wagged his tail excitedly.

They got up the steep slope by going on a special ski lift, which was really like a bench that dangled from a wire. Claude thought that it was a very fun way to travel and it didn't really matter too much if you got your skis in a tangle here and there. You could still admire the view.

SNOWY MOUNTAIN
RULES:
No Running
No One-Man-Band Outfits
and
NO OUTDOOR VOICES

72

When they reached the top,
Claude looked down.

It was **very** high!

Claude squinted through his binoculars. He could see Sir Bobblysock sitting outside the log cabin having a hot chocolate. He was chatting to a nice young man and showing him his bunion.

All of sudden, Claude felt light-
headed. It was probably from being
up so high. He suddenly desperately
wanted Sir Bobblysock to see him
all the way up at the top of the
tallest mountain, so he started to
jump up and down and wave.

Then you'll never guess what he did.

He forgot all about using his Indoor
Voice and shouted at the very top
of his Outdoor Voice:

HELLOOOOO

SIR BOBE

OOOOOOOOOOOOOOOOOOOOOOOOOO
YSOCK!!!!

His voice echoed around
the mountains.

Then there was rumble...
and a grumble...

"Uh-oh," said Claude,
suddenly feeling a bit
hot under the collar.

77

A *huge* sheet of snow slipped down from the pointiest peak and rolled down the slope in a giant ball.

"Avalanche!"

cried Sidney Snood, before he got wrapped up in the giant snowball like a hot dog in a bun.

The other skiers leapt out of the
way, but down at the bottom of the
mountain, Sir Bobblysock was too
busy reading a magazine to notice
the avalanche coming, and...

splat!

The giant avalanche snowball
splattered all over the log cabin.
Sir Bobblysock and Sidney Snood
were covered right up to their
pompoms in cold, wet snow.

"Help!" they mumbled.

There was a big problem.

Sidney Snood was the only Mountain Rescue person, and because he was right at that very moment completely covered in snow, nobody knew how to rescue him and Sir Bobblysock.

Nobody, of course, except Claude.

But how was he going to get
down the tallest mountain on
these silly skis, he wondered?

Then he had an idea.

Off went Claude's skis. Over his shoulder went his ski boots and then he took out his tea tray from his beret and—*whoooooosh!*—off went Claude down the mountain.

He was at the snow-covered cabin in seconds. Now all he needed to do was dig Sir Bobblysock and Sidney Snood out, but how? His paws were too dainty to do much digging...

Claude snapped his fingers.
He remembered Sir Bobblysock's
silver shovel prize. He rooted
around in his beret until he found
it and then he dug and he dug
and he dug.

Snow flew everywhere and poor
Claude's arms ached. Eventually
he managed to dig down to Sir
Bobblysock and Sidney Snood
and helped them clamber up
out of the snow.

The crowd who had gathered
around to watch clapped softly.
"Three quiet cheers for Claude!"
whispered someone.

And everybody whispered in
their quietest Indoor Voices,

"Hooray!"

"Hooray!"

"Hooray!"

Claude went quite pink. Then he poured Sidney a nice hot cup of tea from his emergency tea set and popped Sir Bobblysock in the heated foot spa.

Chapter 8

When Sidney Snood had stopped shivering he clapped Claude on the back.

"What a brave and clever dog you are!" he said. "Won't you come and live in the Snowy Mountains and help me rescue people?"

Claude thought about it for a moment. Whizzing down the slopes was terrific fun, but he liked living in his nice warm house on Waggy Avenue too.

He looked down at Sir Bobblysock.
All the color had gone from his
face. Claude thought they had
better go home so Sir Bobblysock
could put on his pajamas and
recover properly with his hot water
bottle and a box of chocolates. He
explained all of that to Sidney,
who said that he understood.

By this time it was getting late and
Claude needed to get back before
Mr. and Mrs. Shinyshoes came
home from work.

So he put the foot spa under his beret and said goodbye to Sidney Snood. Then Claude and Sir Bobblysock hopped onto their tea tray and skedaddled home through the snow.

Later that evening, Mr. and Mrs. Shinyshoes had a surprise when they came home from work.

"Goodness!" said Mr. Shinyshoes, "I wonder where all this snow has come from?"

"And I wonder why Claude is fast asleep with his feet in a foot spa?" said Mrs. Shinyshoes.

"Well, I'm sure I don't know..." said Mr. Shinyshoes.

But we do, don't we?

*Keep your eyes open for Claude and Sir Bobblysock.
You never know where they'll turn up next.*

CLAUDE.
at the Beach

A seaside holiday turns out to be more than Claude bargained for when he saves a swimmer, encounters pirates, and discovers treasure! HC: $12.95 / *978-1-56145-703-8*, PB: $7.95 / *978-1-56145-919-3*

CLAUDE.
at the Circus

An ordinary walk in the park leads to a walk on a tightrope when Claude accidentally joins the circus and becomes the star of the show! HC: $12.95 / *978-1-56145-702-1*

CLAUDE.
in the City

A visit to the city is delightful but ordinary until Claude accidentally foils a robbery and heals a whole waiting room full of patients! HC: $12.95 / *978-1-56145-697-0*, PB: $7.95 / *978-1-56145-843-*

CLAUDE.
in the Country

When a fearsome bull interrupts Claude's afternoon down on the farm, he must think like a cowboy to save the day! HC: $12.95 / *978-1-56145-918-6*

CLAUDE.
in the Spotlight

Claude is ready for his stage debut—but when a spooky theater ghost tries to ruin the performance, Claude knows the show must go on! HC: $12.95 / *978-1-56145-895-0*